White roses we follow, toward Teller's Hollow

Dead earth to a spring, the house of a king

A sip from the chalice, we enter his palace

Break bread for the Keeper, now we descend deeper

Washed clean in his pool, we fall under his rule

Away from what is, we all are now his

PARADISE SANDS

A STORY OF ENCHANTMENT

LEVI PINFOLD

• First US edition 2022 • First published by Walker Books Ltd. (UK) 2022 • Library of Congress Catalog Card Number 2021953483 • ISBN 978-1-5362-1282-2 • This book was typeset in Futura. The illustrations were done in mixed media. Candlewick Studio, an imprint of Candlewick Press, 99 Dover Street, Somerville, Massachusetts 02144 • www.candlewickstudio.com Printed in Shenzhen, Guangdong, China • 22 23 24 25 26 27 CCP 10 9 8 7 6 5 4 3 2 1

IT WAS DRY AND DUSTY, and it was Bill driving,
Danny in the passenger seat, and Bob beside me in the back.

"We should take flowers. Mom would like flowers," I said.

"White roses we follow, toward Teller's Hollow," sang Bill, laughing.
"Remember?"

"That nonsense," I said, "is nonsense."

And that was how we left the road.

We worked our way along the bank. Soon we had picked a lovely bouquet, but the heat left us gasping.

Farther along the track was a silent building.

"Dead earth to a spring, the house of a king," sang Bill, with another laugh.

"I wonder if we could ask for a drink of water," said Danny.

"We have enough flowers now," I said. "Mom will be waiting."

But my brothers were thirsty. Without another word they made their way toward the quiet building.

I watched them drink deeply
from the spring.

Afterward Bill did not sing, *A sip
from the chalice, we enter his
palace.* He did not laugh.

All was quiet and still. Nobody
seemed to be in.

"I think we should leave," I said.

I called after my brothers as they climbed the stairs. They did not hear me as the door swung inward.

Danny was muttering that he was hungry. Inside was a table laden with food.

Mom's voice sang in a memory, *"Break bread for the Keeper, now we descend deeper."*

"I'm so hot," said Bill
after they had eaten.
"The air is too dry."

I tried to tell them
that the flowers were
dying, that we should
leave, but my voice
disappeared into the
silence. Cool water
beckoned.

*Washed clean in his
pool, we fall under
his rule . . .*

Away from what is,
we all are now his.

I called for help, but my cries were answered only by echoes. I ran from one locked door to another, from hollow windows to empty courtyards. But no help came, so I turned back to the pool.

And there he was.

"Who are you?" I asked.

"I have many names, but you can call me the Teller," said the Teller. "Won't you drink?"

"I don't want to drink," I said. "I only want to leave with my brothers."

"Your brothers have made their decision," he said. "They took what was offered. They belong here now, and they must live by our rules. But you must be hungry. Won't you eat?"

"I will not eat or drink," I said again. "And I will not leave without my brothers."

"Foolish girl," he said. "You would rather starve than be part of paradise? You belong here. A place is waiting, just for you. A wonderful, safe place."

"My brothers and I are part of a family. We belong together, not with you."

The Teller considered, then uttered a long sigh. "Three days," he said. "You have three days. Three days without eating or drinking and things will be as they were before you came here. But if you take any food or water during that time, you will stay. Are these terms acceptable to you?"

I looked straight into his eyes and accepted his terms.

On the first day, there was a
banquet for the residents.

I neither
ate nor drank.

On the second day,
the feasting continued.

I neither ate
nor drank.

On the third day, there was
only heat and the sun.

I neither ate nor drank. But I did give a little
water to the flowers to keep them alive.

As dusk fell on the third day, the Teller returned.

"I am impressed," he said.

"I did not eat. I did not drink," I said. "Now you must keep your word."

"Not just yet," he said. "You did not eat, you did not drink, but you did take water."

"I did not eat, I did not drink," I said. "These were your terms. Give me my brothers back."

"Oh, I will," said the Teller.

And the hotel, the residents, and the Teller all exploded into dust.

I fought my way back to the track, down past the dust-beaten flowers. As I scrambled down the slope to our car, the dust whispered in my ear.

"I will return your brothers," it said. "The agreement stands. You did not drink, you did not eat, but you did steal water from me, and I will take something from you in return. One day your own daughters and sons will visit me here and, if they choose to stay, they are mine."

I wrenched the car door open, and there was Bob asleep. I fell into the seat beside him and closed my eyes.

AND IT WAS BILL DRIVING, Danny in the passenger seat, and Bob beside me in the back. Bob was doing his chicken impression, and the others were hooting with laughter as if nothing had happened.

At last we were there. We went past reception, up two floors in the elevator, and there was Mom. Bob, Danny, and Bill all hugged her in turn.

"We brought flowers," I said.

Mom looked carefully at the flowers, then deep into my eyes. A shadow of something crossed her face. Something like concern. Or maybe an old wound.

"From Teller's Hollow?" she asked.

"From Teller's Hollow," I replied, my voice trembling.

I looked away. We both understood.

And we drove home.